FIRST PERSON SINGULAR

Ross Ulysses Munroe

Manor House

Library and Archives Canada
Cataloguing in Publication

Title: First person singular : short stories / Ross Ulysses Munroe.

Names: Munroe, Ross Ulysses, author.

Identifiers: Canadiana 20190239891 |
ISBN 9781988058542 (softcover) | I
SBN 9781988058559 (hardcover)

Classification: LCC PS8641.L97 F57 2019 | DDC C813/.6—dc23

Cover art: Oneinchpunch / Shutterstock

First Edition
Cover Design-layout / Interior- layout: Michael Davie
144 pages / 22,500 words.
 All rights reserved.
Published Nov. 21, 2019
Copyright 2019
Manor House Publishing Inc.
452 Cottingham Crescent, Ancaster, ON, L9G 3V6
www.manor-house-publishing.com   (905) 648-4797

This project has been made possible [in part] by the Government of Canada. *« Ce projet a été rendu possible [en partie] grâce au gouvernement du Canada.*

*For Virginia,
the Keeper of my Soul*

<u>Untitled</u>

There are the little events in life. And there are the significant events in life. Individually, they all seem to have their place. But what happens when we take them together as one?

A unified picture begins to emerge, much like an impressionist painting, a mandala, a lenticular image, an autostereogram, yielding up an underlying theme that sews one's experiences into a deeper narrative, rendering a profile of the myths we are living out.

It is the Rorschach analysis of our souls. And it has no name.

Table of Contents

The Book of Spirit - 111

About the Author

The Book of Life

Gang Warfare

Currently a trendy neighbourhood populated by Millennials who see their investment more like a cash register than a home, the Annex in Toronto wasn't always so genteel.

This is where I was hit by a car at seven, sending my shoes flying and my pride in tatters. Where my sister was abducted only to be thrown out of the vehicle because she screamed bloody murder all the way down the street.

The objects of some sniggering, this is where we had no grass where the front lawn should have been. Except on every Firecracker Day, when we were heroes as everybody up and down the block brought their cherry-bombs, their ladyfingers, their sparklers - and where burning schoolhouses were the grand finale.

This is where I was chased by the gangs, because I wasn't Italian or black or Ukrainian or because I was younger than they were and my father didn't believe in fighting.

When they caught me, they lit more ladyfingers and threw them down my shirt.

So I got hold of a folding knife with a 5" blade. To spread the word, I showed it to some girls who immediately ratted me out to the crossing guard who immediately called the cops who immediately dropped in to see my parents.

It was obvious I needed another strategy.

Then it hit me and when three of the toughest Ukrainian gangsters-to-be, brothers at that, stopped me in the street for a pounding, I was ready.

"Are you still around here,' one of them inquired.

'Yes but there's a big problem.'

They all blinked, holding off on the punishment. I knew I had bought about five seconds.

'You see, it's my birthday next week and I was planning on inviting you to the party! If we do this, my mother won't let me...'

They absorbed the tragedy of all this. One brother looked at another. He looked at the third. Then they all shrugged, what could they do? They tore themselves away and went in search of another victim.

Of course it wasn't my birthday nor was there a party. But they never bothered me again. In fact, they seemed to put me under their protection, much like a prize cow. After all, there had to be a birthday coming up sometime. And I don't think they were used to being invited to celebrate any of them.

This must have been where I got my start in advertising.

Freight Train

He was 50-ish, black, looked like an overweight fly-by-night entertainer with a big hat. The freight train was picking up speed slowly and he had a big steamer trunk with all his professional & worldly possessions and an accordion.

He ran for the life of him - risking it all - and summoned up the verve to heave that huge trunk up in the boxcar with all his remaining strength.

Then the train picked up its pace and he couldn't get on it himself, left alone and out of steam for the rest of his life as it flew away from him ~

Chalk One Up For the Tooth Fairy

A bunch of us from the office went to the Igloo restaurant for lunch in Baffin Island - including my good friend and fellow band-mate Chris. Now you had to be very careful at the Igloo. It functioned as a parabolic reflector.

You could hear the conversation of the table exactly 50 yards away on the other side, as if they were talking into your ear. Since Iqaluit is a small town, more than one fistfight or worse started that way.

This is a town that if somebody goes home with somebody else's spouse when they're out of town, and there's a blizzard which can block doorways for days, it can lead to much worse, when they can't get back home in time.

People have hacked each other's arms off with axes there for less.

We were all chatting at lunch when Chris found a tooth in his food. He freaked out and called the manager, who had the cook come out. Speaking no English, the cook simply offered a broad grin. He only had two teeth in his head.

Picking his jaw up off the floor, Chris ordered another lunch and all of our meals were on the house. A few free cocktails salved the insult.

Back at work, Chris came into my office. He sheepishly told me to have a look and opened his mouth. He was suddenly missing a tooth.

Pure Jeanius

My brand new Levi jeans. I delivered a lot of newspapers and sold a lot of greeting cards to buy them.

Now, at the age of 12, I was invincible. I could even carry my empty guitar case around for the adoring yet nonexistent crowds with my head held high.

There was a great TV commercial where a cowboy was out on the range and buries his Levis in a makeshift grave, a tear running down his cheek. It was the kind of bond reserved for one's dog when it up and died. And I wasn't allowed to have a dog.

I tried them on and swaggered around my bedroom. Then I tried them on again, and practised smirking in the mirror nonchalantly. After the third episode, I ran out of things to do with them and wondered if I'd misspent my money.

Then it struck me. I could wash them!

Full of enthusiasm, I grabbed my new blue jeans and rushed to the basement to the washing machine, loaded it and poured in the detergent. And I mean poured.

So I fired it up and whiled away the time accepting gushing compliments from people I never knew that never existed. They were mostly girls.

Finally they were ready, just as clean and blue as the day I bought them. No wonder. This *was* the day I bought them.

I put them on and strolled with much fanfare over to a friend's house, salivating over the accolades to come. But he wasn't home. Then I tried a second and a third, to no avail.

I sat on a bench pondering the problem, when it happened. A big juicy raindrop splattered on my forehead. Then another and another. The skies opened up and it was a deluge, a torrential summer thunderstorm completely soaking me from head to foot. Including my brand spanking new, true blue Levis jeans.

They immediately started foaming, bubbles spewing out and down my legs. I made a break for home, but the faster I ran the harder it rained, and the foamier it got, until I looked like I was covered in shaving lotion.

As I raced in the front door and past my father, he blinked a few times, then went back to his newspaper. I half expected to be on the front page the next day.

The Night of the Beaver

I was twenty years of age. I camped out by the Yukon River for the summer (what there was of it), and every day or so my companion and I would blow up our air mattresses and float lazily down to town to do our grocery shopping.

Avoiding the water birds who dive-bombed us all the way to protect their nests, bevies of bees attacking and swarms of mosquitoes the size of fighter jets, we would finally straggle into Whitehorse wet and the worse for wear, then hitchhike back to a warm fire.

After a day in the bush of clearing brush to widen the Yukon highway, we'd join our aboriginal friends and eat: berries and caribou cooked over the flames, a piece of flat rock serving as a frying pan.

Then, to the bonfire party in the bush. With 200 wild spirits ecstatic, dancing and chanting to the drum of the Great Spirit. Hours later, I was exhausted and soaked in sweat, finally turning and trundling towards town. After nearly breaking my neck tripping over logs a couple of times and falling off precipices in the dark a few more, I froze. A shadowy figure was following me.

A wolverine? Even the grizzlies were afraid of them. A timber wolf - a very hungry one? Too slow. Then into the moonlight I saw it. A beaver. A very fearsome beaver. The kind you read about that makes your blood curdle. Except there aren't any of those.

I started to make fun of him with his buck teeth and big fat, flat tail, now slapping the ground furiously.

That's when he attacked. But nobody ever told me beavers could jump. He leapt a full three feet in the air, going for the throat as if it was a tree trunk.

I jumped back and he did it again. And once more.

I turned tail and he did also, wobbling towards the highway and off to the beaver pond to join his mates, in their goal of utterly destroying all boreal forest in the immediate vicinity.

I never took these events too seriously until I read about a fisherman in Europe. He was attacked by its continental cousin, who bit the gentleman's aorta, mistaking his leg for a birch I guess. After gushing over the beaver, the man promptly died.

Results of Fruit Fly Extermination Study

The Following Study was conducted under Exacting Conditions, monitored by the Appropriate Regulatory Bodies, in order to arrive at the most Expeditious Means of Eradicating an Infestation of Fruit Flies in the Premises.

The First Premise - as the Police would term it - was the Kitchen, which was inundated by Pregnant Fruit Flies of the Female Gender.

An Extended Salvo of Rapid-Fire Swatting on my part was met without success, since even one Pregnant Fruit Fly that evaded the Barrage resulted in the Replenishment of the Entire Population within 24 hours.

Removal of the food sources - fruit scraps in the garbage, minuscule puddling of juice on the counter, etc. - proved to be less than Fruitful, since these Little Beggars can live on Almost Anything when required.

Further Study demonstrated that the Fruit Flies were enticed by a cap full of Pinot Grigio and went to Heaven before they Died. But Previous Experiments had shown that they preferred a Good Scotch.

Unfortunately, their tastes are Too Discriminating. Attempts were made to entice them with:

1: Cutty Sark ($20) ...
2: Dewar's 12 Year ($33)
3: Black Bottle ($26) ...
4. Johnny Walker Red ($35)
5: Compass Box Great King Street Artist's Blend ($40)

Not One of them preferred any of these - during our First Tries. So we had to Pony Up for a good Lagavulin 16 Year Old Islay Single Malt Scotch Whisky ($140) - which was immediately Swarmed, as the Fruit Flies indulged in Belly Flops, Swan Dives and Nose Dives to their own Ecstatic Detriment, finally expiring in a drunken haze.

As F. Scott Fitzgerald would have it: 'First you take a drink. Then the drink takes a drink. Then the drink takes you.'

The findings show that the Efficacy of the Extermination is directly Proportional to the Size of One's Wallet. The Facilitators of the Study celebrated this Discovery with a Bit of Lagavulin of their own.

The Big Dump

In this case, I had a shoot supposedly on the fourth floor of a low-grade studio. Usually the crew shows up and wires the place with heavy-duty electrical cables. Then the director arrives 2 hours later to review the wardrobe, set and props, lay out the shot list and coach the talent.

In my own defense I did stop at McDonald's for a number 2 breakfast. Bad choice. When I got to the 4th floor of the studio, there was no crew. There was no equipment. There was no Producer, no talent, no coffee. But there was a toilet, with a water closet right in the middle of the room, where a washroom used to be.

What else could I do all alone like that with no guidance? Afterwards, I saw a handle halfway up the 3" pipe and pulled it to flush. It completely sheared off and water began gushing out, and onto the floor, flowing to the 3rd floor below by the gallon. There was no shutoff valve, but that's not my area.

The contents of the bowl sadly remained intact. In a panic I ran downstairs to the 3rd floor. Water was gushing through and down to the 2nd. I ran down there and the flood was seeping into the 1st. I rushed down there only to find 25 crew members hooking up the electricity on the ceiling prepping for the shoot.

They weren't looking but I was, as the water started bleeding in. I cozied up to the Producer and he said the 1st floor became available, and he'd saved an hour of humping equipment up the stairs. I told him not to turn the power on under any circumstances (since people would immediately die) and to send a plumbing crew to the 4th floor very quickly.

'And tell them to be careful with the toilet bowl, it contains hazardous waste.'

Within an hour it was all settled and we got the day anyway. Meanwhile I had just made the worst entrance of any director on any set anywhere in the world. Luckily, there is forgiveness in this - it is all within the prerogative of the director, who is usually dumping on somebody.

Violin Solo in B Flat

'Will anyone who wants to learn to play the violin please proceed to The Office.'

This was likely the only time I had entered the place willingly. The teacher raised an eyebrow, but let me go anyway and I was excused from class.

And so it began; at first it was enchanting, opening a whole new world of exploration and delight; a universe where I was free, unbounded and full of possibilities. Until my parents got hold of it, that is.

I think they had been concerned about where my life was going. After all, I was already in Grade 5.

For nigh on four years, I tried tiptoeing out of the house after doing the dishes, taking out the garbage, pretending to clean my room, faking my homework and prepping the evening meal.

But I never seemed to be fast enough to pretend I didn't hear those soul-killing words on the way: *'Don't you think you should put in some time practicing your violin before dinner?'*

And so the drudgery would begin again. 45 minutes after school each night enslaved by, *What Child Is This?* and *Waltzing Matilda.*

This, while everybody else was out having fun — throwing mud balls at laundry waving so enticingly in the breeze, attacking wasp nests without getting bitten, chopping down trees for no good reason, shoplifting candy and the like.

I couldn't even tell my friends because it was so unheroic.

What was worse, every time a relative came to visit from Montreal, I had to open the case and draw my bow for their listening enjoyment, making it sound as bad as possible, until they finally caught on and stopped asking. I wanted to grab that violin by the neck and throttle it.

To be fair, there was a moment or two of glory, though, playing 2nd violin in the junior symphony orchestra. Held in a real concert hall with a hundred or so players, a professional conductor and a real audience, we were all infused with sense of destiny, and we weren't too bad either.

But then came the dreaded Kiwanis Festival, since I was really on a roll and still worth bragging about. We had to choose the music to be considered, and my parents picked that old Robbie Burns favourite *Flow Gently Sweet Afton*.

I tried this time, I really did. When we got to the competition, it became apparent that my father was the only man in an audience of sixty or so geriatrics whose husbands must have died, leaving them with a lot of time and enough money on their hands.

Despite my trepidation as my turn approached, I screwed up my courage and stumbled on stage. One shoelace had come undone and it didn't augur well.

The piano player began the introduction, but they never brought me the sheet music. After a few go-rounds, the pianist stopped, while the audience fidgeted. I think they had to go to the bathroom anyway.

After an eternity, the Master of Ceremonies whispered *'You are supposed to play from memory, or you'll be disqualified.'* I was aghast.

I elected to play with the sheet music, but it wasn't an inspired recital. Especially with all those girls looking at me snidely. *'What was a boy doing here anyway???'*

Later, my father acted as though nothing had gone wrong, but it seemed to drag him into a well of disappointment at his own performance in life. I was never nagged about practicing again.

And then I learned to play the guitar, doing songs I actually liked. And the trumpet, the bass, the harmonica, and the banjo, and I developed a taste for singing. Because once you learn one instrument you understand them all.

Which goes to show that you can suppress the inner flame. But you can never snuff it out.

Not Quite Twice Carjacked

Recently, I came within 3 seconds of being carjacked in broad daylight, at Church north of Queen in downtown Toronto, while parking on the west side.
He took two runs at me: The first intending to surprise me from behind while I was putting my parking chit in the car.

I felt him coming up my vertebrae before he did and instantaneously I stood straight up, turning around as he was walking rapidly toward me for a quick hit, now 3 feet away.

But I surprised him and luckily I was 6" taller (yet 25 years older; also luckily I was wearing my red wife-beater - a flag for the bull, throwing him off his game). And knowing how to go low to the ground when it was called for.

I also had the literal and moral high ground by a few inches. 30 years of Tai Chi were very helpful. The center went where it moved.

So at the last moment I forcefully struck his unconscious, with an energy move he didn't understand and he did a silly five-year-old 90 degree move, (which is likely the age at which he was so traumatized that he started to pursue his errant path) - and he turned behind my Mini at the last moment instead and pretended to cross the street.

He was almost struck down and killed; rush hour was coming on. But this was not my intent.

In 2 seconds, the traffic not allowing him to cross, he became even crosser with the world that stood in his way, enraged with himself and with his failure, and he reversed his body, loathing himself and me by association, coming back around straight at me - a scant few feet, lifetimes and moments away.

I leaned back slightly to afford me room for a possible quick kick below the torso, and moved my hands in defense above and below my stomach in case of an incoming knife - it was a case of daylight brashness, and they were positioned to become offensive if necessary, or to effect a fake.

For an eternal moment, delighted now, his consciousness expanded like a peregrine falcon, preparing to strike - something he was clearly bred for. But mine did too and, for a moment to his surprise, our minds fused, throwing him off balance.

I was ready above and below and he realized it.

Sneering, he rolled off to the right around me, his eyes rolling as I rolled with them to make sure he was going. Onto something else.

A similar event occurred to me a few years ago in the afternoon a couple of blocks away by the Flatiron Building at Wellington and Church.

Is this a consequence of going to Church too often?

Wrestling With Death

Nine months ago I vomited a pot of blood, and found blood in my stools.

Over the course of the next little while, I lost a lot of weight, I became extremely fatigued, I had a high fever, and it became difficult to walk. With the medications I was put on, it became problematic to even drive.

Finally, my wife, Virginia, ambulanced me to the hospital and they immediately put me into Critical Care, with a Gastrointestinal infection. I was in the hospital for a month. They say this condition may last a lifetime; it has left my Gastrointestinal tract impaired, but I don't believe them. I seem to be getting stronger.
After a month of intensive care and physiotherapy, they released me. There had been a danger that I could die, and apparently there still is, but who doesn't face that?

It appears to be getting better.

Once in awhile, I think it's a good thing to have a wrestling match with Death. It's good for the soul and helps to clarify matters in the Deep, from which all existence arises.

If you win, the spirit is purified and a thousand sins and misapprehensions are dissolved in the Light. If you lose, you are dissolved in the Light.
But how much needless effort do we expend attempting to wrestle with Life as it works its will on our temporal existence. It is irrepressible.

And it will hound you to the last breath unless you dance with it and smile.

A Big Strapping Mama

When I was seven my mother sent me to the store to buy a loaf of bread.

When I passed the neighbor's place downstairs, I noticed the door was open and their TV was on. I paused to look in. They saw me and invited me in. I spent the next half hour in ecstatic joy.

Then, realizing I was in default, I scampered upstairs - without the bread - to face my Maker. When she asked what happened, her eyes narrowing, I told her.

I watched as the wheels turned in her mind, searching for the correct teaching.
Then she looked me in the eye and said: 'You have two choices. Go to the store right now and get the bread. Or I'll give you the strap and you can go back and watch TV.'

A shiver crawled up my spine. I said: 'I'll take the strap.'

And with every whack on my hand, my soul was liberated. I don't know what she intended to teach me, but what I learned was that if I could withstand the pain, I am completely free of the constraints of this world.

Truth in Advertising

Of course, it has long been fashionable to disparage advertising and other marketing communications as trite and banal, the lowbrow second cousin of real writing,

But if it disappeared, the entire economy would disintegrate with it and all the jobs related to it, causing a permanent global economic meltdown.

Certainly the vast majority of it is rubbish. Some rises to the level of a fine art.

To see it in an even broader perspective is to realize that the vast portion of Nature reproduces through sending signals regarding what it has to offer and what it wants, all the way from insects to sea creatures, birds of flight and land animals.

They are advertising and have for hundreds of millennia. And without that function, there would be no life as we know it...

Holiday Greetings!

The following letter generated many hundreds of dollars at Christmas. So much so that the company called to find out how I was doing it. I never told them...

Hello. My name is Ross Munroe and I am 11 years old. I deliver your Globe & Mail newspaper, but you probably don`t know me, because you are still sleeping when I make my rounds in the morning.

Since the holidays are here, I am leaving you this beautifully illustrated copy of Jeandron Greeting Cards to look at today. I am sure you will enjoy seeing them. Also look at the many gift ideas if you have time. You will like these too.

I don`t have many catalogues, so I will drop by tonight about 7 p.m. to pick it up, along with any orders you may want to make.

Thank you for being my Globe & Mail customer and I have enjoyed bringing the paper every day, except when I forgot to get up in time. Then my Dad had to drive me, even though he was very busy.

Yours truly,

Ross Munroe
Your paperboy

Surprise Attack

It was always best to take them by surprise, early in the morning, just after the summer sun had rolled up over the hill and begun to blink the haze away from its drowsy eye.

The entire colony was still dazed, slow and lumbering from the cool of the night. Four or five sentinels were usually on duty at this time, and even they were not yet quite of this world.

I crept up behind the cherry tree to get a bead on their positions. Stealing a glance around the trunk, I saw the yawning hole that led deep into the centre and down towards the ground. It was about eight inches in diameter and three or so feet up the base.

How it came to be, I had no idea, but this much I knew: Whether carved with the surgical precision of a lightning strike from the heavens or gradually crafted by the patient hand of nature, it was no accident.

The cavern was there to house the colony. The colony was there to challenge me. I was there to rise on Saturday mornings to answer the call. In these times I knew exactly why I was alive.

Around the woody lip were perched three warrior-class ants, each black with a red thorax. That flaming mid-section was proof enough to expunge any nagging doubts I might have had about what was to follow. They were mercenaries, ready to leave their fields for battle the moment the least opportunity arrived for ravage and ruin.

In a body, they could gather and hurl across the grass towards the residence of their lesser, peaceful, black cousins, where they would descend, boiling and spitting, to turn the unfortunate inhabitants into mincemeat.

Then they would pillage, carrying off every edible speck of food (including more than a few dead bodies) and dozens of unhatched eggs, to be nurtured into life and brought up in slavery.

Their heads were slung low to the ground. I looked at the long, curved pincers and shuddered. For an instant, I imagined the little beasts to be all around me, as big as elephants, charging full speed with jaws gaping and slavering …

What terrified me most was that deep down I could sense that they possessed no real malice. It was far worse than that. They were merely efficient, the kind of efficiency that no plea for mercy could ever undo.

In a flash I leapt forth and dealt them to death.

Within the minute, three more ventured out, confused and awkward. A shiver crawled up my spine. How did they know? Three had died; three had taken their place. I could excuse the robot-like efficiency of one tiny ant. He would need to pole vault just to reach for my toenail.

But to know that it spread through to thousands and thousands of little minds that lived deep and brooding within the heart of my beloved cherry tree, that thought towered over me like a thunder cloud.

I was half in fear that this malignant wraith could detach itself wholly from the colony and range down the street at will. Perhaps it already had. I had seen something similar in the eyes of my teachers and others, too.

I was not far wrong to feel that my very life was at stake under the benevolent branches of my cherry tree.

I turned and they quickly joined their brothers. The colony observed two minutes of silence in their honor. I had an idle vision of the inner guard conferring, likely wondering whether to alert the high command.

I looked up, hoping the cherries would be early this year. Two weeks more, with luck. I urged them on.

A dozen ants raced out of the hole, fanning out in search-and-destroy formation.

They knew I was close. I left them to end their run and they circled back, crisscrossing every piece of ground in a disorderly and anxious fashion. My shadow lengthened and they were no more.

More silence. The air was torn by the crack of a branch as it bent before a sudden gust of wind. The humidity hung heavily on my brow, and I, too, began to sweat.

Then they came. They had decided, and it was a flood. Hundreds swarmed out of the darkness and up the trunk, the bark transformed into a syrupy mass of ferocious little bodies, each hell-bent to render its verdict on this early morning intrusion. The entire contents of the cherry tree had disgorged itself in one foul retch and the battle was on in earnest.

I quickly killed 10 or 12 at the base of the trunk, and dozens further up immediately wheeled and raced back down to answer me. They knew. They knew!

Spurred on, I worked furiously, barely able to keep pace, raining blows on the hollow wood like some primitive tribal drummer. And still they came.

They tried to encircle me on the ground. They dropped from branches. They sent diversionary squadrons to the left and right, to distract my attention from the main body of soldiers. It was only by the grace of nature that they hadn't developed heat-seeking missiles, and I knew I had better not give them the time to do it.

They tested me completely and more. Individually, it was no contest, but together they coalesced into a horrific, misshapen hydra, with a thousand biting little beady heads. Where 10 died, 20 filled the space in a single convulsion of my thumping heart. The bodies were everywhere.

I'm sure that one died for every insult and disappointment I had ever experienced, and they were the perfect candidates, too, since I couldn't recognize a familiar face in the bunch.

The second wave came and it was too much to handle. I retreated to safer ground. I picked an ant off the back of my neck and drew a deep breath. It was time to bring up my doomsday weapon: water, and gallons of it.

I poured it right into the gnashing maw of the colony until it filled the cavity, with hundreds of little bodies whirling into unconsciousness. The water level dropped and I did it again, and once more.

They would feel my power deep in the sacred bowels of the kingdom, yes, even at court, where the Queen must now be shaking in her dainty little ant-boots. They flailed impotently in the face of my expanding spirit. With a final belching bubble, the water drained out and they were gone. Even the ants on the trunk and limbs had disappeared.

The little demons also knew when to retreat.

I waited a moment, looking at the bark and up, up to the spreading branches that carried all my summer cherries. For the time being, the tree had been exorcised. There would be little activity for the rest of the day.

I became distracted and gradually ambled away, my mind turning to the remainder of my weekend agenda. Until the next morning, that is.

So it went for more than three years, and while I learned much in the art of war, I was not alone. The little monsters did also. But with the aid of technology and the know-how garnered from many hours in front of the television, I was always able to outwit them. In springtime I could lay in enough firecrackers for a month, and the air was rank with testimonials to the empty heroics of my enemies.

Then one summer morning I was taken. It was a surprise attack, I wasn't prepared.

It was in the midst of one of the biggest pitched battles I had yet endured. I was holding off on the water treatment – I didn't want to end the drama so abruptly. That was a big mistake. I had just obliterated seven attackers charging up the right flank of the tree, and I twisted to the left, where a score or more were digging in under the bark for a stand.

I used my fire thrower: a can of deodorant spray, the alcohol ignited by a butane lighter. It had a range of 14 inches and they were roasted. I turned back to the troops that were pouring out of the colony and stopped short, aghast.

There among the teeming masses was an ant much different from the rest. His abdomen was completely missing, blown away perhaps the day before. He was a war veteran.

It was grotesque.

If he was, through some fluke, still able to survive in sadly abbreviated form, he should have died just out of gentlemanly good taste. Yet here he was, flying across the battlefield on his remaining four legs like a hound from hell.

He looked here, he looked there, chafing to avenge the monumental insult I had inflicted upon his clansmen – and yes, I thought, upon his own sacred body.

Then at once he froze, and seemed to glare right up and in to my eyes, while his comrades scurried obliviously around him.

I was convinced that he recognized me. I stumbled backwards and fell to the ground, the weight of 5,000 massacred ants suddenly brought forward and pressing on my conscience.

He could feel! They all could feel.

The sky was spinning away from me. For the first time, it was I who was whirling in the water and rushing deep into the mouth of the cavity towards unconsciousness, joining those I had sent before me.

Twenty minutes later I could stand, but I couldn't remember if he'd lived or died. I hoped he'd lived. Nor could I find him among the survivors busy cleaning up the carnage. But in that one short moment, I had realized just who it is that lies hidden in the humble form of a red and black carpenter ant.

And after three years, it was the ants who won. I never went back to that tree again.
Except, of course, to eat the cherries.

'More Cowbell!'

The sound of hundreds of cows rising through the mountains in Switzerland was almost as inspiring as the energy flowing up the spine.

The gentle echo of cow bells was rising everywhere through the valleys to heaven.
And when I drove into one valley and called some of them over, they gathered around me in a most serious manner.

I think they thought I had the inside track with the farmer.

I gave a political speech with great gusto: they stared without blinking. They taught me that day ~ how to be a politician without being hit by cow pies.

Birth

I recall a hanger trying to scrape me off. I've had an apprehension of them ever since. And there seemed to have been a lot of flushing of various sorts.

But I still would not have voted for Kavanaugh.

Blood. Poo. Bodily fluids. Coughing. The invasion of air, an utter violation.
Then the wrestling match came.

Blood. Slime. Poo. Just like life. She was no pushover, and she was teaching me a lesson.

She fought me and I fought her. No she said. Yes I said. I won. I am here. I became strong very quickly. My thick Taurus neck still hurts from the force of it. It was a good prep school for what was to come in life.

They didn't have money to pay the hospital bill, so my father sent in a friend to sneak me out under a raincoat. He told him if he was stopped to cite Habeas Corpus.

My father had told her she had to give me up once I was weaned, since he didn't want to commit. Even though my grandfather was a multimillionaire way back then.

Perhaps that's why he gave me the middle name, Ulysses, because he knew I'd be sailing over many waters and it was his favourite poem by Tennyson. It was 40 years before I read it, and it fit my life to a tee.

So six months rolled by and that day came. When I was being dropped off like a sack of dirty laundry, she held me close and said, 'You wait for me. I'll come back for you.'

She secretly came to see me every week. 'You wait for me. I will come back for you.' She didn't want me to lose hope. And I believed her. In the foster home I contracted dysentery. She had me moved several times.

After six months she bought me new clothes she had no money for, and then told my father she wanted to show him something. She brought him in to see me, and I reminded him of one of his relatives it was said.

I wonder which one.

So he agreed to take me home. Because they weren't married, they used to hide me in the closet when company came over. Possibly with a shot of whiskey to keep the secret where it belonged. I was too old to fit their story.

Because I was a love child, they decided that anything goes, and never cut my hair for three years. They liked those long red curls. I felt like Samson.

When I was up half the night in pain because my legs were cold, she would gently pour a warm bowl of water and bathe my feet. When I was beat up by older boys in the neighbourhood, she would storm down and pull them off and kick their butts.

A misinformed advisor said with great gusto 'Ross, your father gave you away because he loved you.'

Meanwhile, this was a woman of great character, and she never got much credit for it. I cried when I wrote this. This is the core of my pain and my blessing. I bear no grudge. We all need both these things.

Some Ad Agency S.O.B.

A Partnering Agency flew up from the States in prep for a big pitch. After the strategic planning session, we were all having a glass of wine in the boardroom.

That's when he started to brag.

Apparently, he had been pitching against a legend in the industry the year before, whom I knew of, but shall remain nameless.

This was a prolific creative genius and a gentleman. He was getting older and walked with a cane. But it was known that once he hobbled in, he blew the doors off everything else.

So this idiot waxed on and on about how he won the account.

He had called the man's airline and cancelled his plane tickets. Then he called the man's hotel and cancelled his room reservations. Then he called the client and cancelled the meeting.

He giggled his head off.

Universal Codependency

I just realized that the entire universe is codependent. It must need a lot of therapy, we might have to do an intervention.

Extreme Weather Alert

Under no circumstances:

1)   Take an herbal laxative before sleep as recommended

2)   Arise in the morning when the sun is doing the same

3)   Do a body cleansing meditation

4)   Juice some beets, carrots, celery, cucumber, pears, apples, lemon

5)   Have oatmeal, blueberries & bananas

6)   Then go do a Tai Chi set on the beach

Just don't do it.

Superman Flies High

I was 16 and I sold 30 hits of purple microdot to a friend in Grade 12 on a Friday. At only $3 a pop.

He seemed happy, but I didn`t know that he resold them.

Meanwhile, on the Saturday, it was Halloween. My friends were all getting together for a costume party, and I was still alone in the apartment dressing up as Superman, and I'd ingested one myself.

I was ready to go, cape and all, when there was a knock at the door. I opened it.

Down the stairs were a dozen very nasty looking bikers lined up on the stairs, looking up at me.

Apparently taken aback by my costume, it took one of them a few moments to clear his throat and spit it out. 'That LSD you sold us was fake!'

I would have thought my costume would have been enough to disabuse them of that notion.

Realizing my psychological advantage, I held up my pointer finger. 'Wait right here - I'll be right back!' They looked at each other, confused - but nodded in assent.

So I closed the door, and flew through the apartment, down the fire escape and off to the party.

My friend put everything right on Monday. I suppose the microdot kicked in for them.

Regarding Fishing & Polar Bears

I lived in Frobisher Bay for nigh on 3 years, played in a rock band & managed an Energy Conservation program just before my Saturn Return.

What fishing!

And the ice floes when they showed up suddenly in the morning were like angels - or European ships - appearing from nowhere with their hues of alabaster.

I cross-country skied across the bay until I realized the next stop was Sweden.

There were as many polar bears on Baffin as people at the time. They can run 40 km. an hour and swim at 10. And they do like people a lot.

That made me run like hell on a fishing trip to the Interior whilst wandering too far from camp.

A Grisly Encounter

My employer up there in Whitehorse told me many stories about his encounters with Grizzlies as a guide. A hunter who was behind him after firing a shot, was attacked, the bear ignoring the guide, turning the offender into dead meat.

He said they have a double skull that bullets glance off of. And fat that absorbs high impact shots. And a double fur configuration that snares incoming projectiles.

We were burning bush to widen the Yukon Highway. Somebody had to stay on the site overnight to make sure the fires didn't get out of hand. And it paid overtime.

I'm a half mile from my pickup truck, tending the dozen piles of fires. I heard a crashing ten feet into the woods, parallel to the highway and growling. Saplings were going down by the dozens.

There's something uncanny in a visceral way that occurs in the moment when your life is on the line. Time slows to a crawl. Your senses expand. Your intelligence is multiplied.

Now a Grizzly can do 35+ miles an hour on open ground and more going up a hill due to their massive haunches. They say they can smell you dozens of miles away.

Either he had a nasal condition or I did the fastest half mile in history.

That's when I understood that this is not my life.

The Hungry Vegetarian

We go into an organic meat store and after looking at the fare, ask the butcher how to best prepare this chicken, Parmesan-style.

He smiled and said he didn't know. He's a vegetarian. But he was out of work, so he took whatever he could get.

The Ungrateful Civil Servant

It was an uncommonly cold winter day, but I was determined to get my ticket reduced for being late on a red light.

$375!!! We could do better than that.

So I bundled up with my wife, put on my faux fur Trapper's hat, and headed down to court to beg for mercy.

When we arrived, it was apparent we'd be a while. The line was long and the proceedings were going very slowly, even though the building was cold.

Fortunately, I had my lucky Trapper's hat to assuage my discomfort.

I waited patiently for the law clerk, who wore a hajib covering her head; with her lack of command of English, it was clear she hadn't been landed for long.

'Take off your hat!,' she yelled at me from across the courtroom. When I looked at her confused and at her headdress in surprise, she coiled up and struck again. 'Take off your hat! You are in court!!!,' she bellowed.

Well, I didn't want to lose my case, so I complied. But I think she missed the irony of the whole situation.

After all, in my books my fake rabbit hat is a symbol of ethnic pride and reverence. Especially when the air gets frosty.

Highway To Hell

We were a-gumbootin' her down the frozen bush road at 70, my '67 crank-start LandRover fishtailing all over the ice, an hour from the job site, my dozer and the doghouse where the coffee was brewing.

Suddenly, the vehicle lurched violently, smashed from behind and careened off into the bush, its momentum broken by the 3 feet of snow in there, finally grinding to a halt after running over a dozen saplings and narrowly missing a few tree trunks.

It rolled over and the crew spilled out - just in time to see one of our fellow crews speeding off down the highway, giggling with glee. This was their idea of an early morning joke.

We flipped the 4x4 upright, pushed it onto the road and set off in pursuit of our revenge. It was going to be a long day.

The Wheel of Life

Today we got attacked in the car by a drunk guy in front of Old City Hall wielding a bicycle wheel. The traffic was in gridlock so there was nowhere to go. At first he threw it at the car ahead of us, and it landed standing up against the driver's door.

When the driver didn't get out to remove it, I got out & did it myself, stupidly throwing it back on the sidewalk out of the way. When the assailant realized who his real enemy was, he lunged toward me.

The closer he got the bigger I looked - and the faster I moved to the car.

And just after I locked the door, he stood in front of the hood, weapon in hand. I jerked the car into gear, implying I would run him over if he didn't stop brandishing the weapon, but he didn't flinch. The courage of liquids and his heritage. Of course, I would have been charged with attempted murder.

You aren't allowed to use a bigger weapon than your assailant.

He hit the windshield with great force twice with the center of the wheel, but it bounced, then the hood. $500 damage, now covered by insurance, what with the police report. Then he inadvertently dropped it to the side, fortunately, and I was able to skin around him while he retrieved it.

As we sailed on, I saw him in the rear-view beginning to work on the car behind us while Virginia called the cops. If all the men in all 20 cars had just got out, He would have been getting help in 30 seconds, and so would all of us.

Dear Smoking

You tart. I have loved you. Oy - so what did I get?

45 years of sucking up, choking, endless demands for money & unwarranted attention. Burns. Brown fingers. Carpet burns and holes in my favorite shirts. You're the worst I ever had.

When smoked, with the other hand though, you did get me through some challenging times. So thanks. And goodbye.

I used to love you, but it's all over now.

Attention!

Once, some years ago, in an ad agency, I got a call
from a head hunter. She said
'I don't understand what my client wants.'

I said 'What were his actual words?'

*'He said - 'find me the writer with the shortest attention
span you can'*

I said 'You just found him.'

Then he hired me and we won a bunch of business &
awards. It's emotional-intelligence martial arts.

You have 2 seconds to not think.

Horror Show

The day was done, and my buddy said everybody was going to the Friday Night Drive-In. This was where the guys who had them took their dates and the ones didn't took their angst.

Once the car was parked, I noticed something odd. Most of the vehicles were turned away from the movie screen and towards one of the cars.

Everybody's attention was riveted on it, and looking closer, I saw a guy crawling slowly along the ground towards the driver's door.

In the wink of an eye, the interloper lunged towards the door like a panther and yanked it open. He dragged out the driver, who was just putting the moves on his date, threw him on the grass and began pounding his head in.

The driver's date was a former girlfriend.

And it was just another Friday night's entertainment for everybody in the oil patch.

Raping a 25-Pound Cat.

I was working as Energy Conservation Manager in Baffin Island, designing & supervising the retrofit of a solar/wind demonstration house as well as conducting energy audits on 400 buildings there.

Counter-intuitively, solar was economical because the government shipped oil in by tanker for use in the hydro plant, with a very low efficiency rate. What's more, the land is covered by snow a good part of the year when heat is in demand, which results in the reflection of solar energy onto the collectors. Being evacuated tubes, the heat loss was minimized.

Now up there, things can go sideways. Someone I know was evacuated himself for vacuuming up the snow in his underpants.

There was a cat down the hall that weighed 25 pounds. I know, because when I saw him waddling down the carpet, I brought him into the apartment and put him on the scale.

One day I pressed the elevator button and when the door opened, a man was on the floor trying to rape that cat.

He was so drunk and passionate that he had taken every stitch of clothing off. The cat, of course, had no clothing at all. When the door closed I pressed the button again, in disbelief.

With this confirmation, I reported it to the owner, who called the police. The fellow was arrested when he went to the hospital with extreme lacerations to his groin. As they said, it could have been a child.

A Spider Bite

As an 11-year-old, having a bath, a spider dropped on my stomach from the ceiling, he must have lost his footing. Or I looked a lot smaller from up there, perhaps like quarry. And, startled, I almost moved to kill him.

Then I thought - why would I do that: I'm so big, and he's so small.

Then he bit me. Hard. Then I killed him immediately. Thank the gods it wasn't in the nether regions.

An Irish Wedding

This was my most important direct client, and I had worked on the account off and on for ten years, winning awards across the globe.

In the most recent run of work, I had labored on the account for four years, when the marketing director I reported to was fired, and replaced by a new client.

After a bit of finagling, I got into his good graces, and since their office was two thousand miles away, I was able to present all the work over the internet, thus eliminating any static that might have arisen through personal contact.

Until he flew in for a meeting. Which led to drinks at the bar and dinner, of course. As the evening wore on - and I mean wore on - he shedded his Teflon veneer, and from beneath it emerged a pompous, bellicose, nasty, vindictive, egotistical, snot-nosed, arrogant, overbearing twit.

He also had his bad side.

This is a guy who thought it was fun at dinner to text other people at the table, suggesting that they ditch one person who was also at the table - one of his other suppliers. After slogging through our own evening, I breathed a great sigh of relief when he flew back home.

"That's awful," my wife said to me in sympathy, "but don't worry. You won't even have to see the guy again for another four months."

The next morning he called to announce he'd be back in town for dinner and drinks within a couple of weeks, and that he planned to make these evenings a regular occurrence.

I think he liked to get out of the office, as well as enjoy the complimentary Chianti, and Steak Diane. This went on for a year, and I was always on tenterhooks, worried that I would lose my cool and the account in one angry outburst.

This is why creative directors and copywriters have account people to manage the client in large agencies. Unfortunately, I was not a large agency.

But I must have done okay because - to my absolute horror - he invited me to his wedding.

In Ireland. How could I refuse?

Fast forward to the Emerald Isle. My partner and I had been settled into a quaint Bed & Breakfast in the Irish countryside, with our client staying with his fiancée's family just a blarney stone's throw-up on the road.

At the end of an afternoon of quaffing Guinness and scarfing down barf-food, while listening to interminable tales of his witty exploits and brave adventures, I escaped back to our B & B for a nap, only to hear a commotion downstairs as my client came in with his suitcase.

'I've been getting pretty tired of all those women up there, so I'm moving in with you guys for the week.'

At the wedding, we realized why we had been coerced into attending. His Irish wife had 120 guests at the celebration. He didn't have a single friend there. His best man was a distant cousin. To my client's credit, his divorced parents did attend.

'I was going to have my best friend fly over and become my best man. But for some unavoidable reason, he had to cancel.'

No kidding. To be kind that's not the half of it.

Once we returned home, I was able to hang on to my temper for a few more months, before firing him as a client.

Now, you may be the kind of person who simply loves gadding about town with someone you don't know and don't like, who holds the Sword of Damocles over your head. If so, the opportunities for you in this world are almost limitless.

Please don't ask me to join you.

Information as Delusion

The exponential expansion of Information as delivered through technology asks each of us essentially 'What does this all mean?':

Thesis: Information is a diminishing commodity, contrary to common conception.

It has been useful in recent history, but only a tool. Yet given how increasingly prevalent Information is through all media, it actually impairs clear thinking. Information is only relevant when one considers who is defining it as such, otherwise it's gobbledygook. And that it is Information at all is based on who is watching it & what their motivators are.

Currently, information is a product - often a distraction - sold by certain people, with an objective. Too much of it, and it clouds the faculties.

The question is: Where did it come from & from whom? Are there hidden agendas? Why is it useful, promoted by & to whom and what is its intended purpose. It's simply a tool, but like one, it gets manipulated, for better or worse - like fire. Fire can cook food; but it can burn fingers, depending on who uses it and for what.

Information of its own accord ignores its own right to exist - it presents itself as unbiased, in order to serve one's objectives. But Whose?

That makes it Not Information

Where's The Party???

It was the end of a 14-hour day scarring the landscape with my D9 Cat Dozer, dropping 12" gas pipeline in the trenches. After cutting the engine, the last cloud of black smoke belching up the stack, I was invited to a party by my mates. A party of sorts.

Host: *You wanna fight?*

Me: *No, but I have a question.*

Host: *What?*

Me: *I've only been here an hour and I've been asked for a fight three times.*

The host leaned back on his heels and he gave me a long, searching look.

Host: *Where're you from, boy?*

Me: *Ontario.*

He leaned in with a toothless grin.

Host: *Well - in Ontario, you ask a guy you just met out for a beer. Here we ask him out for a fight. It's just our way of getting to know each other real fast.*

Then I ducked.

Saturday Night Fever

It was just another Saturday night. We were speeding along 82nd Street, racing against every other crew cab to make the next red light for no reason. Everybody got there at once.

Suddenly the two vehicles in front of us disgorged their contents and six strapping roughnecks got out, baseball bats in hand.

They smashed the windows, the lights, even the mirrors, glass flying everywhere.
Then the light turned green and they all jumped back in, speeding off to the next red light.

Girls are hard to come by up there.

Castration Day

On our day off, my buddy took me to his family farm for Castration Day. That's when the greenhorns get turned into no-horns. Here's how to do it with an Elastrator and a Burdizzo Nipper. Some Nipper.

Use this technique when the spermatic cord can be palpated - one month and older.

Choose and use the proper sized forceps for the size of animal. With undersized forceps, there will be too much tissue between the jaws and there will not be enough force to properly crush the arteries.

Find the spermatic cord on one side of the scrotum. Reach between the hind legs and grasp the scrotum above the testicles.

The spermatic cord runs from the testicle into the calf's body. It is about the size of a pencil and moves easily from side to side in its half of the scrotum.

Pinch the cord to the outside edge of the scrotum between your thumb and forefinger. If right handed, use your left hand to hold the cord and your right to operate the Burdizzo.

Position the Burdizzo correctly for crushing. One jaw of the Burdizzo has projections at each end to keep the spermatic cord from slipping out of the Burdizzo.

Place the jaw with the projections on the front side of the scrotum. Point the projections toward you.

Include only the part of the scrotum that contains the spermatic cord between the jaws of the Burdizzo. Do not crush more of the scrotum than necessary. The jaws should be placed just above (1-1.5 cm) the top of the testicle.

Close the Burdizzo, count out 10 seconds and check to be sure the spermatic cord has been held between the jaws of the Burdizzo. You can also rock the spermatic cord back and forth in the jaws.

Release the Burdizzo, move it to a new site 1 cm below your first site, and repeat steps four and five. Choose a site below the first crush to minimize acute pain from a second crush.

Repeat the procedure on the opposite side. Stagger the pinched areas on the left and right side of the scrotum. Do not pinch a part of the scrotum that lines up with a pinch on the opposite side. The crush lines must not overlap the centre-line of the scrotum (Figure 4).

Check calves four to six weeks later to be sure the testicles have shriveled. The testicles swell initially and then degenerate and shrink in size.

As each bull was heaved down the sluice, it was grabbed by the hind legs at the bottom, eyes rolling wildly. During the castration, each would emit a low, plaintiff, mournful wait, as if to say 'Oh no! Now they're cutting my balls off.'

Personally, I would have put up more of a fight...

Holy Shoot!

A wacky shoot we did for a week at Silver Star Mountain in B.C. - Ken Davis, Producer, who has since passed on, Martin Julian DOP, me Writer-Director.
I lost 5 pounds in the latrine before getting on the glass-bottom chopper, such was my anticipation. Marty was hanging from a harness below the helicopter. shooting.

I had two headphones on - one to call the camera underneath me & one to cue the talent on the ground, who Ken managed. For dramatic effect, we had to fly in over to reveal the scene, as close to the trees as possible.

While up there I thought - 'If we crash & die, it'll be the best possible funeral...such notoriety' At the time I actually felt it was only up to me to decide, as the Director of my life.

A week later, another crew went down & perished in a ball of flames there.

How to Get a Job in the Middle of a Recession

ok. So it's a deep recession and I arrive back in Dundas, Ontario from out West, having driven bulldozers, earth scrapers, steel rollers, rubber-tired pavers in Alberta & Saskatchewan, worked in the mountains on the railroad on Vancouver Island, on the oil rigs etc. - when there wasn't a recession on.

I'm 24, ok, so I went to a bar to meet some old buddies.

On a Sunday, they look at me bleary-eyed and asked what my plan was. I told them I'd just go get a good one. 'But they only pay minimum wage, if you can even get one.' They winked at each other then smiled.

Ok, the next day I drove up the hill towards Hamiltonia. And I thought, there are no jobs in Hamiltonia for a guy like me.

So I turned onto the Highway adroitly named The 403, which was unironically transformed into the Royally-Named Queen Elizabeth Way.

But this Way was, even though magnificently going East, obstructed, obfuscated transgressed and diminished by what some lowlife, bureaucrat and petticoat-chaser called the Her Least Highness #427. Her 427 luck was about to run right out.

I turned North, as I sensed at an emotional level that there were no good jobs downtown there for a guy like me. But when I got to the Highway named by the Ancients as The 401, I thought, there are no jobs for me beyond this point. So I went East. As far East as a 24-year-old adventurer could in those days. All the way to Kennedy Road. In Scarberia, an ancestor of what Years in the Future was to become Greater Torontonia.

Well, once I saw that the sign that AjaxOnia was bashfully sidling up, I knew it was time to get off this unproductive non-joyride.

So Kennedy it was. But I knew in the pit of my smaller gut at the time that there were no jobs further South for a guy like me in that nonnuclear desert, so I turned West at the first intersection even though they had never heard of Timmy's, had no stoplight nor any current redeeming feature at all. This path led to a partially constructed dirt road, a shadow of its dirty old yet unarrested self.

I rolled over a hill on the road and it abruptly ended at a small cliff, confronted by a large undeveloped woodland. Fortunately I put the brakes on.

I thought, what am I doing looking for a well-paid job in the boonies 50 miles from where I started out in the middle of a recession in Scarberia? I turned the car off and considered what this meant.

I looked to the right to see a dozen beginnings of houses, just framing themselves up to consume whatever inhabitants they could gobble up. Predators are patient as they lie in wait for their quarry and the traps are set for life.

I looked to the left and there was a steel roller with the name of the company - Andrew Paving - and the phone number below the logo. I called the next day and was hired at three times the prevailing rate.

Over a beer later that week, my buddies asked me how I could possibly have done it in the current economic situation.

What could I say? Not this. Not that.

Great Friends Who Died

Peter Barrett Burns

Jim Brown

Ken Davis

Keith Tarswell

Roger Mayne

John Board

David Reppen

BeatleMania

I sold more Globe & Mail subscriptions than anyone else that year, so I won the Grand Prize. A ticket to see The Beatles. One single ticket. It kind of defeated the purpose.

I don't know where they got it but it was at Maple Leaf Gardens, so my father had to drive me in from Hamilton. He had me dressed up in a suit, because that's what you do when attending a concert. At least that's what he did when he was younger.

He dropped me off at the arena and I immediately realized the error. Everybody else was wearing faded bell bottoms and sandals. Everyone else except, of course, The Beatles themselves.

When people stared at me, I simply pretended I was with the band and they got out of my way quickly.

Afterwards, he asked me how it was and I expressed my rapture convincingly. But the seat was buried so far up in the rafters and the screaming was so loud, I couldn't hear anything else. I didn't tell anyone at school the next day though.

And secretly, I learned never to trust his judgement again when my public image was at stake.

Caribou Love

A gang of us flew into Amadjuak Lake in the middle of Baffin Island via Sea Otter on a fishing trip. I had flown my Dad up to boost his spirits in a midlife crisis. The plane landed on the rocky shore and dropped us off.

We all set up our tents, started the fire, broke out the fishing gear and cracked the whiskey.

Now Amadjuak Lake is big but it's almost completely landlocked, freshwater with cliffs running along it. So any Arctic Char that make it in through the rivers from the ocean can hardly get out again. As a consequence, there's not much to eat except each other.

Although there are some 15-pounders, many of the others become deficient with great big heads and jaws and spindly scrawny bodies. And when you throw a lure in the water a dozen of them make a beeline for it like U-boats in the North Atlantic.

We had a bet on - $200 for the biggest fish. I cast out my line and immediately caught a 3-pound Arctic Char. But he was being chased a by 15-pounder. I yanked him out of the water and tried to disengage him but I couldn't.

In frustration, I took the whole rig, fish and all, and flung it up on the shore. Then I grabbed a buddy's rod and started slapping the water and caught this interloper in five seconds.

I shouldn't tell you what brand the lure was but anything would have sufficed. Cha-Ching! It paid for my airfare.

The next day out of boredom I wandered a mile out of camp swatting the water. Then I remembered that there are as many polar bears on Baffin as there are people and ran back like hell.

The next day we noticed a male and female caribou slowly wandering across the tundra grazing. One of our group ran to get his hunting rifle. I asked him how he could reconcile killing such a magnificent creature when he couldn't create one.

'We're allowed to take the male. Just not the female, she might be pregnant.' You don't argue with a guy like that with a hunting rifle in his hand and a bottle of whiskey in his gizzard.

So this pastoral couple took 30 minutes to chew their way across what grass there was, looking up to blink once in a while and flick away the flies. When they got close enough my camp-mate lined his 30-06.

I shuddered to think how the female would react to what happened next.

The shot rang out, echoing across that barren wasteland. The male dropped like the 400 pounds of now dead weight that he was. The female looked up alertly. For about five seconds.

Then she went back to chewing the grass without even a lawyer to represent her. It took her about an hour to wander over the horizon.

She never looked back once and was never cross-examined. Is there a learning in this?

Kiss-Off

Everybody in Grade 7 was always talking about Marion. Blonde. Blue-eyed. With boobs!

They said she went to the back alley one day with some older boys in Grade 8 and took her clothes off until she was starkers.

It probably wasn't true. But if you were 12, it seemed like a really big deal and I desperately had to have her.

I told my friends 'I will meet her in the back alley after school' though I had never said a word to her before. Nor even looked her in the eye. I don't think she knew I existed.

Word was spreading and I enjoyed the notoriety for a few days, until the actual day arrived. An intermediary arranged that we would meet in a garage and proceed with the business at hand.

At the prescribed time, I began walking down the alley with a friend. Trudging, really. First there were five of them waiting to see what would happen. Then seven more, peeking around corners and over fences.

I turned a corner and there were forty or more, as if to witness a gladiatorial contest. They all stared at me, speechless, as if I was a sacrificial lamb going to slaughter.

The crowd parted and there she was, an offering to Eros and Aphrodite, performing a sacred ritual we would all carry with us to The Elysian Fields.

I paused and she froze. The air was laden with anticipation. If I could have laid this burden on one of my schoolmates I would have. It was not to be. There was a hush all round and I advanced slowly, leaning towards her, and planted a great big kiss on her Rubenesque lips. It lasted at least ten seconds.

She didn't pull away. She didn't even wipe it off. And I think I inadvertently brushed her breast, though I couldn't be certain. I certainly bragged about that to my mates later.

The crowd let out a collective sigh. Her entourage began to evaporate and drift away and so did mine. But the deed was done, and we all had taken a journey together.

All without uttering a word.

Suicide By Seagull

Larus Argentatus. They're known as the Rats of the Air. Screeching. Fighting over every French fry. Defecating on picnics.

Once I threw a bunch of buns in the lake, and watched as 25 of these wretches zoomed in and brawled over one of them, ignoring the rest of the buns until they had created a whirlpool that sucked them down and out of sight.

So greedy they are that they have dived through the air and hooked themselves while snatching fishing lures during casting and had to be cut free.

But we needed one for a commercial shoot, though using them is illegal. The spot was being produced for Mariner Outboard motors, which had a 'spotless' reputation for reliability .

It featured a seagull that danced atop the motor to the music of a lounge singer scat singing (No pun intended).

The commercial ran: "Mariner Outboards have a spotless reputation for performance around the lake. Well...almost." Then the seagull winds up and dumps on the machine.

The 'lake' was filled with water - really a tub with a painted backdrop. The motor was placed in the lake. And the animal handler brought out the star of the show - who began diving headlong into the water to get away.

After 20 takes, the bird never came up again. It was a clear case of Seagull Suicide.
But the handler wasn't about to give up so easily. He struck out to get seagulls from his 'secret stash'. Three hours later, with the crew now on overtime, he returned sheepishly.

Apparently he had three seagulls in a cardboard box when his car broke down. Going for help, he couldn't leave them unattended by the side of the road with all the transport trucks flying by, so he carried the box up an icy hill and set it down.
As he left, a gust of wind grabbed the box and sent it sliding down the ice on the hill and onto the highway, where it was promptly flattened to resemble a pancake.
Nothing but feathers remained.

Once we all finished grieving together, the handler called in an Illegal Seagull Specialist and we got the day without making much more of a splash.

One, Two, Free!

Ok, it was utterly politically incorrect. If I'd done it today, I'd be flambéed and lambasted. A car rental company was offering the third weekend to students free if they rented two in a row.

My headline was *One, Two, Free!* Not exactly a work of genius, but it was the right thing to do. Anyway, the radio was going to be much more fun.

It opened on an English-as-a-second-language class filled with Asians, to whom the instructor was trying to teach what the phrase meant.

Except the students would have none of it.

After a bit of wrangling, the students explained the promotion for the edification of the teacher — that they could get a third rental at no charge, after paying for the first two.

The Agency bought it, the client agreed, and we were into production in the sound studio. What could go wrong???

The talent laid down their tracks with a bit of coaxing. The stock music was dropped in. And we sourced background chatter of the class from the sound library for atmosphere. Then we all went home, satisfied that we had nailed it.

Until the commercial aired, that is. And the phone at the Agency was ringing off the hook.

Apparently the voice talent that did the background work had had a little fun of their own. Since whoever produced the stock sound effects library didn't know any Asian languages, the voice talent threw in every expletive they could think of.
It went to air as recorded and caused an uproar that echoed across two continents.
The Asian community boycotted the company. The recording studio was fired. The Agency lost the account. And I kept my head down.

Other than uttering some very foul language of my own.

Love Potion #1

There were obvious clues. But she was so good-looking and she hadn't had sex in months. So I turned a blind eye, And I let her collect me like a butterfly.

She wanted to go to Europe and stay in only the finest hotels, something she did regularly and alone. *'Who knows — we might even get married,'* she said with a wink.

But her temperament would flip like a light switch. Like when I wanted my $3000 back to cancel the upcoming trip and she tried to run me over with her Jaguar. I was walking down the street by way of an escape and she came speeding around the corner.

I had to dodge her Vandem Plus four or five times before she satisfied herself that I wasn't going to hop a fence to get away.

She screeched on the brakes with the vehicle sliding sideways to a stop and leapt out onto the road tearing her clothes and ripping off her non-faux jewelry.
Just ten more minutes of anguished histrionics, and I got back in the car. Europe it was.

After all, she was so good-looking...

Love Potion #3

We were bombing along the highway at a precipitous rate, attempting to make Amsterdam by nightfall. There is hardly a speed limit on the Autosnelwegen.

We got to the city late and scrounged around for a hotel, settling on one and negotiating our way through the maze of parking signs, every nook and cranny having been already spoken for.

Of course I don't read Dutch. Exhausted from the drive, we flopped into bed and slept the sleep of the angels. In the morning, with the sunlight streaming in, she coaxed me into going to the car and getting some coffee.

Except when I got there, there was no car. All of them were gone, and I had learned to read a little more Dutch than I'd known previously.

When I told her what happened, she hit the roof of the cab all the way down to the pound. By the time we arrived, it had become an adventure in a foreign country.

The front gate was wide open, and we decided to try making a quick getaway. There were two nice Sri Lankan gentlemen who tried to distract the Dutch. They helped her occupy the officials by pretending to throw a brick through the window.

Amid all the hubbub, I sneaked into the car, fired it up and hit the gas. I didn't know they had a spring-loaded barricade embedded in the pavement, and they triggered it at the last moment, hanging the vehicle up with tires spinning.

It must have triggered something in her also, because within a few seconds, she was standing atop a table in the dispatcher's office, swinging a handy baseball bat and challenging them to take her down.

She yelled, she screamed, then she did the inexcusable. She called them a bunch of Nazis and they don't take kindly to that in Amsterdam.

So they rushed the table en masse, dodging the flailing bat, and hauled her off to a cell. After cooling her heels for a few hours, they let her out with a warning.

It was in Dutch though, so I wasn't certain she got the message. Meanwhile, the Sri Lankans had stolen our passports and disappeared.

Love Potion #9

So, of course, we moved in together — into Gordon Lightfoot's old farmhouse. What else was there to do? She hired me away from the agency I worked at. But she couldn't pay me, it was for the good of the cause.

She demanded that I quit smoking, and I had to retreat to the sanctuary of my car to indulge. That's when she took a 2"x4" to the vehicle and grabbed the keys, after giving it a good bashing.

She wouldn't let me see my friends or family and I obliged, to keep the peace. I lost 50 pounds. I looked like a belly button hooked to a spine. She started throwing pots and pans and pulled a kitchen knife.

I called the cops, but she tore the phone out of the wall before I could finish dialing.

I had consigned myself to a sudden death somehow, it was a slippery slope and I couldn't get off it. But when I realized I might kill her instead, I knew I had to leave. I waited until she went to visit her parents, then called a photographer friend.

She phoned while we were loading my stuff into his car and begged me to wait until she got home. But it was a 2-hour drive, so I knew I had a good head start, even with the packing.

I felt I had atoned for a thousand sins, been liberated from a hundred lifetimes of learning, and was as fresh as a new-born baby.

The next time I saw her, I had walked into the wrong recording session. I had gained the weight back. And she was smiling like the Cheshire cat

I walked out again as quickly as my legs could carry me.

Burial at Sea

Who would have imagined that so much vitality and verve could be packed into a simple polyvinyl chloride box. Only 4" x 6" x 4", the cremated contents are often sealed inside a plastic bag. It was black, of course.

Vivacious, immeasurably talented, full of energy and full of beans, my step-daughter, Aurora, had suddenly come down to this.

While the memorial went suitably, we hadn't decided what to do with the ashes. We pictured a glorious scattering over the water at sunset with family and friends. Good wine & hors d'oeuvres. Testimonials. And a string quartet soothing away the evening hours and our personal pain.

But we just couldn't bring ourselves to do it. So she lay in her PVC grave for weeks until her younger sister began to become uncomfortable. At that point, I was nominated to perform the ritual myself.

So I gathered up the package, got a kitchen knife and marched down to a secluded spot at The Beach. Once there, I laid her body down and began reciting incantations and homilies, working up the gumption to open the box for consignment to the deep. I had a teaspoon at the ready.

Except the box wouldn't open.

Gently I pried it. Carefully I prodded it. Then I tried cutting the PVC tabs to no avail. I hacked and sawed and jammed and jimmied, finally opening up its secrets. Inside, a block of ashes looking like cement, and just as heavy.

It was covered in cellophane, so there would be no 'sprinkling' until I cut it open, which I proceeded to effect. Just as a gust of wind came up, blowing the powder all over my person.

Enraged, I threw the entire resting place, contents and all, into the drink, where it likely still lies buried today. I turned and started trudging back home, my kitchen knife dangling at my side.

It was eliciting a few too many open-mouthed gasps and people began sneaking away from me, so I dropped the evidence into the water. Oddly, nobody even notified the harbour police.

The Waterfront can be a real rough place.

How I Killed Jerzy Kosinski.

It didn't have to happen like this and I didn't mean to do it. It was manslaughter. I simply went to a lecture by Jerzy Kosinski.

Of course I had read The Painted Bird - either written by or ghost-written for Kosinski - told from the perspective of a young boy during World War II. He is accused of being a Jewish or Gypsy stray struggling to live during this chaotic period, although Kosiński's narrator denies being Jewish.

To evade the Germans, the boy goes awandering, and the narrative chronicles his encounters with peasants engaged in all forms of sexual and social deviance such as incest, bestiality and rape, as well as other acts of extreme violence.

Then there was *Being There* and *Reds* and many more.

He defected from Eastern Europe to the West by creating a fictitious foundation, then writing recommendations by fictitious Party luminaries attesting to his loyalty.

Once in the New World, among other pursuits, he was given to dressing up in disguises and crawling the streets of New York City, surrendering to whatever adventures lay in wait.

So I went to a lecture by the man himself, recounting his many tribulations and victories. Taking questions afterward, he turned up his nose as he answered the least vacuous, while his estimate of his audience seemed to plummet.

There was a long pause, tailor-made it seemed. Tentatively, my hand snaked skyward and Jerzy pointed to me.

"Given how much misery and depravity you have witnessed, how have you found the strength to carry on in your everyday life?"

At first, it looked like he was going to choke to death. Then he stumbled with his words, and finally meekly spat out, *'I don't know. I ask myself that every day, and every day the world becomes more dreary...'*

A few more questions, and then he was off.

Jerzy Kosinski died by suicide shortly thereafter on May 3, 1991, by ingesting a lethal amount of alcohol and drugs and wrapping a plastic bag around his head, suffocating to death. This was a fashionable way to go at the time.

His suicide note read: 'I am going to put myself to sleep now for a bit longer than usual. Call it Eternity.'

For my part, I could hardly sleep at all, knowing I had been complicit in this crime.

87

The Book of Dreams

Tectonic Plates

I am standing on one of a series of small tectonic plates, about 60 feet across each, which are floating over a huge orb of magma, thousands of miles in diameter.

There is a gap separating each plate of about twenty feet. I go here and I go there, but I can't really get anywhere, hemmed in by the fractures.

I crawl up to a fissure and look down. Far below, I see rivers of magma flowing. Energy is radiating upwards.

I try to jump, but am barely able to catch the other side with my fingers.

Laboriously, I drag myself up to rest. Then fearful at first, I summon the courage to place my hand into that energy radiating from the deep.

It is immediately repelled and no harm is done. I try it again with the same result. I stick my leg in and it rises back to safe ground.

I think without thought, wind up - and jump fully into the gap. The energy cushions my fall and gently raises me back on Terra Nonfirma.

I get the idea.

So I take a running jump headlong into the abyss only to be redeemed. I let out a huge laugh and begin racing across the plates, not giving a hoot about whether I land on land or in the pit, bouncing in and out at random - with great joy and on to infinity.

Retaining the message on awakening, I begin to apply it in my life. For better or worse...

Highlands

I am watching in the Lowlands as Scottish and British troops are marching in good order in full regalia, colors flying, drumbeats driving them. My good friend's grandfather was the head of the Canadian army, the Queen Mother stayed at his cousin's house in Hamilton and I envied him that for some reason. In this dream, I wonder about my own family.

Then a thunderclap echoes from above.

Suddenly, I hear bagpipes wailing, spilling down from the starving Spartan Highlands. The ground begins to tremble with ferocity.

I look up as thousands of Highland warriors stomp down from the hills through the valleys, feet shaking the ground. At the head of these legions is my gentle father, with 1000 years of documented family history behind him - The Black Watch a part of it, having fought the Vikings, the British, each other, the Germans, the Russians and everybody else - often for money.

Those below make way out of simple good sense, as my ancestors take the field and join the parade, assuming their rightful place. My heart swells.

No wonder I am half Barbarian.

The Chrysalis

An old woman is in the mountains, struggling through a blizzard, waist-deep in snow. Over the ridges in the valley, she can see the welcoming lights of a village far below the snow line.

But she is too exhausted to continue and falls into the white powder.

I say 'But you will be reborn.'

I open her blouse and her breast is soft and young.

She comes alive, losing decades of burdens. She stands and begins to stride with the force of Aeolus down the mountainside toward the village.

With every step, the tears fall away. And she is renewed.

Hare Krishna

I see the Hare Krishna dancing in a reverie, but the scene freezes. I see a dog about to eat a struggling pigeon, but the scene freezes. I see a friend about to jump off a precipice to his death, but the scene freezes.

A shadow-being beckons to me and says 'Behold!' Invisible energy ripples across the ground and into the Hare Krishna, the dog, my friend, animating them.

The Hare Krishna begin dancing again. The dog eats the pigeon. My friend jumps to his death.

Let those with ears, listen...

How I Got Completely iPhoned

They were a pretty good client as clients go. I had produced a dozen or so TV commercials for them over the years and they were looking for a big idea. So I went into the boardroom and presented it: renaming the product The iPhone.

This was before Apple's iPhone and I knew it would be big. I told them to trademark it in Canada and the U.S., but being risk-averse, they balked and decided to stick with their existing name.

So we shot some other spots. But eight months later, I noticed their packaging had changed to reflect their new name. 'We thought about it and decided to go with it.'
And iPhone it was.

Just two years later, Apple came out with the same name and my client had to defend the trademark in court. Contrary to my guidance, they hadn't protected the name in the U.S. They always were a bit on the cheap side.

'How can we defend ourselves now,' they groused. 'Apple has millions, they'll crush us!' So I gave them the plan.

'Buy airtime in all the cities along the border and run the living daylights out of the TV', I advised them. 'Their investors will lose confidence and they'll cave, without going to court.'

'But you owe me 10% of the sale when they buy it, ' I added. To which they agreed verbally. And my client won, for millions. But I didn't find out until Apple launched about 18 months later.

When they denied it, I checked back copies of the business press and the story was confirmed, with the proviso that terms were kept secret. That had been my undoing. When I dropped by their offices, they had moved to much bigger, more palatial ones.

'No, we didn't make any money,' one said. 'Not much, anyway.' That's when I had the dream. The two partners were pirates on the open sea. They had a chest full of jewels, gold and silver.

When they saw me coming, they shrugged and threw the whole thing overboard, laughing. As they sailed away, sometime later in the distance, I watched as they pulled on a chain. Lo and behold, the treasure chest was attached to it and as they brought it back aboard again I realized I was out of luck.

I'd been iPhoned.

The Weight

I see my father. I am 9 years old. He is trudging down the road carrying a heavy sack that is weighing him down.

I call out, wanting to help him with his burden, but he can't hear me. He begins to slow down, then stops and lays the sack on the ground to rest, short of breath. Then he dies.

I open the sack. I am inside it.

A Shaman's Teaching

I am sitting with a Shaman. He asks if I want a vision of the Truth. I agree and fall into a swoon.

Suddenly a basketball pro jumps on my stomach. A wolf howls. And the blue moon comes up with a dove flying across the firmament.

I come out of the swoon and the Shaman looks at me with a glint in his eye. 'Everything you have imagined will come to pass. Just because you thought it.'

Then a basketball pro jumped on my stomach. A wolf howled. And the blue moon came up and a dove flew across the firmament. That was enough to really wake me up.

And I immediately had a massive enlightenment experience. The universe atomized itself, exploding into little bits of joy from one non-end to the n'other.

I heard the voice of God laughing, the echoes cascading throughout existence. Then he said:
'Baby Man! Look not for the end. You are just being formed. There will be time enough for what you seek.'

I was in a state of total bliss for five hours while the universe faked itself into reassembling itself in front of my eyes. From that dream, I awakened three times.
No mind-altering ingredients were used before or during these examinations.

Filmmaking

I am with my best friend. We have made a 35mm movie and are in the film house, pitching them on picking up the cost of the post production, for a credit and share..

They vacillate, and my friend doesn't push them, for fear of ruining his future prospects in that regard.

Suddenly the floor gives way, and a canyon appears in the boardroom table between the two of us. One path on his side of the rocky wall leads to level ground. He takes it.

The path on mine leads deeper into the canyon, which widens and has no bottom. I take that one.

When I awaken from this dream, I understand that we are no longer fellow travelers and, although we go through the motions for a while, our partnership is over at its core.

He dies a few years later.

A Mouse in the House?

I am a mouse. I am six years old.

At home, dinner is being served. There are a number of plates. I am watching from about six feet above, in mouse heaven. All the plates are filled, except mine. The Server hesitates, about to plate mine, but forgetting who it was for.

Then she puts the plate back in the cupboard instead. I cry out that it is mine.

But nobody can hear.

Alligator Love

I am lying in bed. I am five years old.

I am holding my plush stuffed alligator. I am afraid of the night and am hoping the alligator will keep me safe, because of its gaping mouth and long carnivorous teeth.

But it is asleep. I am tentative. Because I know that if it wakes up, it will tear my throat out. At least, that's what the other ones tried to do.

Blood

I am naked on a beach. I unscrew my right foot and detach it, to detoxify it. It has healthy red blood filling it, I can see this because the foot is constructed of glass plates.

I decide to remove the plates one by one to get to the truth, all beautifully sculpted to contain the essence of existence. I gently remove a dozen of them and set them aside carefully on the sand.

Suddenly, not much is constraining the blood and it all spills, and is soaked up in the sand.

I can't get it back.

Secret Treasure

In the dream, I am standing in front of my parents, who are seated at the kitchen table. I have probably done something wrong.

Such as being alive.

They are examining me closely for telltale signs. I am 11 years old. Finally they look at each other and take a deep breath. 'We have something to show you.' They get up and take me to a hidden closet, opening the door and flicking on the light.

They wave me in alone and wait. Only I can go in, it is forbidden to them. The room is much bigger than I imagined. It is lined with shelves, seven deep. On each shelf are a dozen ceramic figurines. Each is contorted by a different emotional state. Fear. Anger. Pride. Envy. Greed. Torpor. Delusion. Pride. And more.

I look at them all with fascination. When I turn to face my parents outside, they say 'These are all the experiences we have helped to draw out of you. They will be touchstones to carry with you as you go forward in your life. Treat them as sacred treasure.'

Tarzan Lives

In the dream, I am being afflicted by witches and goblins, overwhelming and pecking at my soul. I am 5 years old and I cry silently. Then I cry out loud but nobody comes.

I realize I can only resolve this in myself, where the attack is occurring.

I imagine being in a dense jungle. I am Tarzan, swinging through the trees. A dozen lusty Janes are chasing me, using vines in the forest canopy. The witches and goblins are nowhere to be seen, and there is joy abounding everywhere.

Evil Warlord

An evil warlord controls the universe.

His eyes can turn and see everywhere. But he is asleep at present.

I have a mission. In my leather pouch are 12 clear quartz crystals and one green one. I begin to plant the clear ones in the ground in a circle on the Sacred Mountain.

As I put them in one by one, he slowly awakens - disturbed at first, then angered, then enraged. I know it is a race against time until he locates me, but I cannot hurry.

Once the twelfth has been inserted, he begins racing toward me. Just as he is about to arrive, I slide the green crystal into the center of the circle. All the crystals are activated together, energy beams pulsating between them.

The warlord is atomized. The world is freed.

D.O.A.

I am walking down the road. I come upon a car accident. The two vehicles have been blown to smithereens, flames still flickering and licking the oily metal. Looking around the scene, I take it all in, aghast.

Slowly, up my spine, creeps the realization that I was one of the drivers. I am dead.

Wake-Up Call

I am in the middle of a dream. The phone rings. I'm not sure whether to answer it, but I do. Then I wake up.

Rearguard

We are wending our way up through the mountain pass, 20,000 of us, exhausted, sweaty, bloody from a hundred thousand cuts by a Samurai force five times our size.

We must make the castle in time to prepare its defence during the impending onslaught. But I will never lay eyes on it again.

Our pursuers are gaining on us, and as we reach the crucible of the bottleneck at the top of our escape route, we glance behind, the invading army close on our heels, preparing to put the hammer to the anvil.

The pass has narrowed now to a scant few feet, and the remainder of our troops scurry through to temporary safety. I alone will be left behind as a rearguard and I test the mettle of my swords, and bow in prayer.

Then they come.

A blade cuts up towards my throat, only to be parried by my katana. Another stabs at my midriff carving a superficial wound before the attacker is dispatched. The blows grow in number but the pass is too small for them to maneuver and the bodies pile up.

I draw my second sword and chew through the maelstrom like a buzz saw through butter, matching blow for blow. As my body and mind are fused, I am invincible.

I only need devote my complete attention to this one timeless moment, unblinking, immaculate and spotless.

This is why I came here. This is what I must fully realize before I leave. I awaken from the dream.

Awakening

Last night. My car was a bit dysfunctional.

When I stopped to check it out, I noticed the trunk had come off its hinges. My passengers said we might miss a great weekend we were on our way to, so I started trying anything I could think of.

- Bungee cords.
- Wires.
- Mechanical hypnosis...

Then I thought: 'wait a minute - this is just a dream'

Then I woke up and the problem was solved ~

Trout Bait

It started as a dream. I was looking deeply into the River. There were the biggest trout lumbering around deep down there. Four feet long and 100 pounds apiece. I stood up and went into a somnambulist state.

I grabbed my rod and fishing tackle and stumbled from the studio down to my Honda Prelude. It was 5 a.m. and the sun was threatening to come up. I had a boardroom presentation downtown at nine.

So of course I had to drive 30 miles northwest until I reached a conservation area with a river running. There was a gravel parking lot and I pulled up and put the car in neutral, grabbing my gear. I was still half asleep and the lot looked flat, so I neglected to engage the parking brake.

Salivating now like a grizzly as the blood started pumping to my stomach, I saw a wire framed stone retaining wall. It rose about three feet above the river rushing below. I dropped the line in the water with salmon spawn eggs on the hook.
I knew I was in business and was at it with joy and laetitiae for about five minutes. Then I felt a very slight nudge behind my knees.

Since I knew there was nothing behind me, I took a step to the very edge of the river, concentrating intently on the matter at hand. 30 seconds later I felt the same thing, more insistent this time.

I turned around to my Prelude trying to push me into the river and attempting to land on top of me and force me to cancel my meeting through the flimsy excuse of death. I only had one second to act. I spun around, dove madly into the river and swam downstream like hell.

I surfaced just in time to see my beloved car teeter over the wall and crash headlong on its nose with buns up kneeling. I don't think the trout were amused.

Recovering my nonsenses, I crawled out of the river. It was now 7 a.m. and cars were starting to fill the roadway to town on the way to their toil. I went to a nearby farmstead and asked to use the phone. I called the police.

Looking out the window, I saw a car pull over every two minutes, the drivers rushing out to see who had died. There was something funny about this.

It was like being a guest at your own funeral.

So the cops came and I explained what happened with my fishing equipment and no blood alcohol content as evidence. So they called a tow truck. Making his nice insurance report, the officer said 'Well the windshield is cracked!'

I said 'Well, it was cracked before.' He said 'But the bumper is almost falling off.' I said 'Yeah it's been like that.'

So when the two unnecessary tow trucks arrived, the owner said 'If you sign this paper that we towed your car back to the city for the insurance guys, we won't charge you anything at all.' The cop agreed.

Now the traffic was getting heavy and I had a presentation to give at nine, after a quick change of cool clothes. Everybody else on the highway just got out of bed.

I just got out of the Credit River.

The Book of Spirit

Life Before Life

At the age of 62, I may as well say it, only having a scant 15 or so years left to recant.

In a deep Primal Therapy session at a cellular level: I was in a deep state of contemplation in an Energy Pod. This lasted for a very long time, but not in Earth years.

I was approached by a male and a female Associate, both of whom asked me if I was ready. I said 'Yes', even though I didn't believe.

I was taken before the Great Spirit, even though I didn't believe in him, who communed with me, and blessed me.

With great fanfare, I was carried down on moonbeams and rainbows, with angels singing, barbershop quartets crooning, and jazz music - to begin first by making all my mistakes and sometimes continuing to do so.

I heard my parents having sex, and entered into this incarnation at the moment of the height of their passion and my conception.

'I AM HERE!'

And it's been an uphill battle ever since.

This is my truth, which I have withheld for more than 35 years. No cult was involved in the crafting of this message.

A Black Cat Crossed My Path

Our black cat, Sara, died a year or so ago after supervising us for 22 years. Here's one of the things she taught me.

She would demand to go outside into the garden at night and wander off in search of insects and raccoons and other cats to investigate and harass.

When I wanted to go to bed, I would open the sliding doors and call her. Of course she never came. Then I realized that I could faintly make out features in the garden, once my night vision came into force.

Except for that black emptiness that was always sneaking around.

And because I couldn't see her, I knew exactly where she was, and could collect her for the night. I was gratified I was not a mouse.

Now I know to look for, first - that which I cannot see.

Since she has currently disappeared from view entirely, I don't see her everywhere I look.

And my heart is at rest.

Stoney Creek Dairy

Peter. He was one of my lifelong friends. Until he died.

He had the heart of a lion. Smart. Funny. A philosopher, an intellectual. A man you could talk with and laugh into the night. A realist, so he supposed.

He didn't drink, smoke or have any other vices that I knew of. Except overeating. Seriously overeating. They say this is the worst of those.

He loved parties, but always hung out at the edges of the crowd, where people would gravitate towards him because of his gravitas. I don't know why but he always followed my lead, he seemed to want a general, someone unruly, or some social glue or something.

Later when he was dying he told me he was just shy. That his worst fear was to be trapped in the center of a crowd of friends even though he brought hundreds together - and threw his shoulder behind a lot of our productions without considering benefits.

He said he was an atheist, but I knew he was lying.

His brain couldn't overcome his heart. After all he had gone to Catholic school, which I never had. My parents had me taken out of class when they recited the Lord's Prayer. But I had since discovered my faith many years later, having met the Divine face to face.

So after many discussions with Peter over the years, I made him an offer he couldn't refuse.

Now one thing about Peter was he was extremely parsimonious. He would go out drinking all night and only order water, then leave no tip. His goal was to put J.J. Mugs out of business at the all you can eat lobster Sunday brunch.

'Peter', I said: 'since you don't believe in an afterlife, I wager something. If I'm right about there being life after death, you have to take me for an ice cream cone at the Stoney Creek Dairy after we've passed on AND YOU HAVE TO PAY FOR IT!

If I'm wrong, you have lost nothing, other than a pound or so.'

Later, when he got really sick I said 'Whatever doesn't kill you makes you stronger.'

He said: 'Unless it kills you.' Then he died.

Now he's out there on the edge of the crowd, waiting for all of us to join him as usual. And he'd better pony up that ice cream or there'll be hell to pay.

A Question of Existence

I always had a mole on my right forearm. But as a kid, I spent a lot of time outdoors in the sun, running through the wood and on the beach. Working on the railroads, and driving bulldozers, paving rollers and on the oil rigs, I got a lot of sun.

The mole got darker and changed, but I'm a guy, so I ignored it. Then a few years later, my older brother noticed it and suggested I have it looked at.

So I went to the doctor and had it removed. He said it was probably nothing.
Two weeks later, I was in the boardroom in an ad agency presenting to clients, when I was asked out to take a call from the doctor.

He said 'R...ross - you know that mole I removed? It's melanoma!!!' He was in an abject state of terror. His primary practice was in GayTown, so I guessed he'd had a lot of bad news over the years and he himself had been traumatized.

Thinking about my presentation in the boardroom, I asked 'How long have I got?'

'You may have a number of years, Ross...' So we scheduled a surgery to remove a bigger part of the afflicted area, and I went back to the boardroom.

Two weeks later, I went into day surgery. It took about a half hour, and when finished, the surgeon said 'I tried to cut the biggest piece I could without grafting, so the scar may be a bit strange. Come back in a week and I'll take the bandages off.'

No kidding. For the first two days I thought nothing of it.

On the third day, when I looked in the mirror I noticed my hair was falling out. On the fourth day I saw with horror that my gums were receding. And plants and insects were dying all around me. On the fifth day, I couldn't get an erection, even alone.

That's when I knew this all had to stop.

I asked myself 'How could this be the best thing that ever happened to me?' After hours of inquiry, the answer came. 'Ross - Use this question physically visibly carved into your body to ask yourself every day whether you are truly living an authentic life. Because if you're not, you're dead already.'

And when the surgeon cut the bandages away, I stared in disbelief. The scar was in the precise shape of a question mark. Complete with the dot at the bottom.

Over the next day or so, I had the most sublime experiences, opening in each moment to the wonder of existence - and the one who watches it.

That was 33 years ago and I still wear it with reverence to this day.

Rite of Passage

And in the twilight of that day, a star shall descend into my sightless eye, the spirit shall spill across the many waters.

And I shall be called GrandFather.

Wave Hands As Clouds

There has been a learning in this for the past 35 years for me and I'm just getting the hang of it

1. Opening of Tai Chi

2. Left Grasp Bird's Tail

3. Grasp Bird's Tail

4. Single Whip

5. Step Up and Raise Hands

6. White Stork Spreads Wings

7. Brush Knee (left)

8. Strum the Pie Pa

9. Brush Knee and Twist Step (left)

10. Brush Knee and Twist Step (right)

11. Brush Knee (left)

12. Strum the Pei Pa

13. Brush Knee and Twist Step (left)

14. Chop with Fist

15. Step Up, Deflect, Parry, Punch

16. Appear to Close Entrance

17. Cross Hands

18. Carry Tiger to Mountain

19. Whip Out Diagonally

20. Fist Under Elbow

21. Go Back to Ward Off Monkey (right)

22. Go Back to Ward Off Monkey (left)

23. Go Back to Ward Off Monkey (right)

24. Flying at a Slant

25. Step Up and Raise Hands

26. White Stork Spreads Wings

27. Brush Knee (left)

28. Push Needle to Sea Bottom

29. Fan Penetrates through the Back

30. Turn and Chop with Fist

31. Step Up, Deflect, Parry, Punch

32. Step Up to Grasp Bird's Tail
33. Single Whip

34. Move Hands Like Clouds (five times)

35. Single Whip 36. Reach Up to Pat Horse

37. Separate Foot to Right

38. Separate Foot to Left

39. Turn and Kick

40. Brush Knee and Twist Step (left)

41. Brush Knee and Twist Step (right)

42. Step Up and Punch

43. Turn and Chop with Fist 4

44. Step Up, Deflect, Parry, Punch

45. Right Foot Kick

46. Hit Tiger at Left

47. Hit Tiger at Right

48. Right Foot Kick

49. Strike Ears with Fists

50. Left Foot Kick

51. Turn and Kick

52. Chop with Fist
53. Step Up, Deflect, Parry, Punch

54. Appear to Close Entrance

55. Cross Hands

56. Carry Tiger to Mountain

57. Whip Out Horizontally

58. Parting Wild Horse's Mane (right)

59. Parting Wild Horse's Mane (left)

60. Parting Wild Horse's Mane (right)

61. Parting Wild Horse's Mane (left)

62. Parting Wild Horse's Mane (right)

63. Left Grasp Bird's Tail

64. Step Up to Grasp Bird's Tail

65. Single Whip

66. Fair Lady Works Shuttles (left)

67. Fair Lady Works Shuttles (right)

68. Fair Lady Works Shuttles (left)

69. Fair Lady Works Shuttles (right)

70. Left Grasp Bird's Tail

71. Step Up to Grasp Bird's Tail

72. Single Whip

73. Move Hands Like Clouds (seven times)

74. Single Whip

75. Creeping Low Like a Snake

76. Golden Cock Stands on One Leg (left)

77. Golden Cock Stands on One Leg (right)

78. Go Back to Ward Off Monkey (right)

79. Go Back to Ward Off Monkey (left)

80. Flying at a Slant

81. Step Up and Raise Hands

82. White Stork Spreads Wings

83. Brush Knee (left)

84. Push Needle to Sea Bottom

85. Fan Penetrates through the Back

86. White Snake Turns and Puts Out Tongue

87. Step Up, Deflect, Parry, Punch

88. Step Up to Grasp Bird's Tail

89. Single Whip

90. Move Hands Like Clouds (three times)

91. Single Whip

92. Reach Up to Pat Horse

93. Cross Hands to Penetrate

94. Turn and Kick

95. Chop with Fist

96. Brush Knee and Punch

97. Step Up to Grasp Bird's Tail

98. Single Whip

99. Creeping Low Like a Snake

100. Step Up to Seven Stars

101. Retreat to Ride Tiger

102. Turn Around to Sweep Lotus

103. Draw Bow to Shoot Tiger

104. Chop with Fist

105. Step Up, Deflect, Parry, Punch

106. Appear to Close Entrance

107. Cross Hands

108. Closing of Tai Chi.

How to Overcome Writer's Block

As Woody Allen said about his stand-up comedy, he doesn't know what he's going to say until he's already said it. In other words, the comedy is not being created by him; it is coming through him. The same way the blood flows through one's veins, the same way air moves through our lungs.

The key is to trust in the process. The universe abhors a vacuum, so all you have to do is:
Brief yourself on the background
Establish what the single most important message is
Form an intention to solve the problem
Then leave an empty space – a vacuum, for as long as it takes

Your unconscious will fill in the content if you give it space. Because it's not about you. You are just a thoroughfare along which the vehicle of the unconscious travels.

The longer you can hold the energy of emotional intelligence in your body without doing anything about it, the better the final product will be. It will insist on expressing itself, much like an overdue bowel movement. Just let the energy rise up your spine and tease it by ignoring it until it is insistent and unstoppable.

As long as there are no stoplights, barricades or other obstructions, the universe will do what it does best - which is to create, perfectly and in the path of least resistance.

If you don't believe that, all you have to do is look around on a glorious Spring day as the cherry blossoms are exploding all around you.

Here's The Very Simple Process:

Review any background documents
Create a document with a title which the unconscious can regard as a receptive space
Stop thinking about it, do other things: a workout, a walk, a swim – make a space of at least a day or two, if possible
Then sit down and splatter any ideas that come to mind while staring at the empty page, without being judgemental – either with them or with yourself. YOU are not the one who is doing this. It is coming through you
Once you have a sufficient number of ideas, go back through them with a critical eye and work with the ones that seem to have merit, polishing them until they become pearls
Remain open - some of the ideas that seemed silly at first may lead to amazing ones, once you revise them a bit

That's all there is to it. You don't have writer's block because you are not the writer. No matter what the voice in your head is, it's just a function of your illusory idea of yourself, not who you actually are. It is attempting to close the floodgates of life that are flowing through your consciousness as surely as the blood is flowing through your veins.

So Ignore These Ones:
· "I don't deserve it."
· "I'll never be able to do it."

· "I'm not good enough."
· "Nobody gave me permission to do it."
· "It probably won't be any good."
· "I'm just faking this."
· "I have no idea what I'm doing."
· "This doesn't make any sense."
· "I've never seen this before, so it can't be good."
· "I'm not getting paid enough for this."
· "There isn't enough time to do it right."
· "I don't feel like doing this right now."
· "I can't do this."
· "I'm not really sure I want to be doing this anyway."

All you have to do is ignore these voices, take a deep breath, go for a walk, have a shower, eat lunch - and come back to the project with a fresh mind. And the good news is, you can come back to this project with a fresh mind every second of every minute of every hour of every day.

What that means is, you can come up empty-handed on getting a great idea 99.9% of the time, and still deliver a dozen good ideas on schedule. You simply have to be willing to let go of any personal pressure or expectation, and let the unconscious work its magic.

Psychodrama

It was a chance to clear long-held energy states and emotional traumas. I looked around the room at the dozen or so participants, silently casting them as characters in my psychodrama.

I had no idea what the plot would be and that was half the fun.

People were not allowed to talk, only to make noises or sing. The story developed as I chose a cast according to whim. The Savior, entreating for the salvation of my spirit. The accusing Prosecutor, demanding I be flung into Outer Darkness. A chorus of Angels chanting alternately in rapture and moaning in despair.

And finally, a proxy for myself, whose soul hung in the balance as the case was made for and against me.

I fiddled with the actors until their positions were just right, then began the play. The Prosecutor hurled taunts and invective. The Angels began intoning. I stepped into the center of the human mandala and the drama began to unfold.

I was brought low by my failings. I was raised by my victories. And slowly but certainly, I started to float, elevated with help from my comrades until I passed muster and was admitted into Heaven.

I wasn't even a Believer, so I wondered where that all came from, emerging from the Unconscious whole and fully formed. In fact, my inner orientation began to transform, as I realized the ascendency of Love over Truth. After being thoroughly enveloped by the experience, it came to an end. It was time for a Sound Bath, then another dreamwork session. Busy, busy...

Death by Scallops

I was hitchhiking to Newfoundland with my erstwhile girlfriend and stopped for the night at a Quebec City hostel, a glorious building, a former jail - La Bastille. Large, strong, European, hundreds of years old.

There were hundreds of bunks in there, most all in one room. They were kind enough to feed us scallops donated by fishermen from the St. Lawrence river.

Scallops past their prime.

But at the age of 17, I was hungry and ate a heaping helping and fell on the bunk fast asleep.

Later, when the dorm was mostly quiet, I was awakened by a voice across the dorm. 'There are demons that come through the walls after me. I am pursued wherever I go. This is a sickness I cannot escape from, they are coming for me now again.' I woke my girlfriend up to hear it, both of us chuckling.

Then I fell asleep for a few hours and woke up with the worst case of food poisoning. I wanted to die, heaving and sweating. The pain was excruciating.

After an hour in hell, I passed out. In the morning, clammy and pale, I left with my fellow travelers.

The man who had spoken in the night came up, looked me in the eye and said: 'How was your night? I guess you will think twice before making light of a Royal Prince of Darkness.' A shiver went up my spine that hasn't left my body since.

Scallops. to this day, are the only food I am deathly allergic to.

Hari-Kari

Now in many earlier cultures, it has been play-acted out as a ritual, a rite of passage, the shedding of a snake's skin, initiating the personal transformation to a new phase of life, leaving the old one to disappear in the dust.

But when the concrete reality of suicide looms, it's an entirely different matter.

* * *

I am 29 years old. The bridge looks down on a busy four lane highway. Cars are roaring along the road, thirty feet below. I am standing in front of the cement guardrail - it's about twelve inches wide – doing surreal, ritual-like movements.
I slowly move through an unbalanced and disoriented perversion of the Tai Chi, arms floating through the air, the motion exaggerated and dance-like. My feet touch down on the railing, almost going over the edge.

I twist and retrace my movements, nearly falling over again, making no effort to prevent it. This continues for a few moments. A car whips past me on the bridge. A teenager leans out the window.

'Jump! What are you waiting for???'

I look at the car as it races off, then back down at the highway below. I stop a moment, staring off with glazed eyes. Then I close them and start to take a step, teetering in the air, unseeing, uncaring. A voice startles me. I open my eyes.

'Excuse me!'

I look down the road. A strange man is trundling across the bridge. The man is completely oblivious to my impending fall.

I step down to the pavement and face him: 'What???'

The hobo hobbles up, huffing and puffing. His clothes are torn and filthy. One foot has a ratty old running shoe on it, with a toe sticking out. The other is wrapped in a dirty bandage, causing the man to limp along in some pain. He appears to be about fifty-five years old.

'Could you tell me if this is the way to Grimsby?'

'What?'

I sit down on the railing, facing him, disoriented.

'Grimsby. Which way is Grimsby?'

I point in the direction the man has come from.

'It's back that way.'

Wouldn't you know it? Walking all night, and the whole time I've been going the wrong way!'

I look down at his disabled foot.

'It's over thirty miles.'

The hobo scratches his stubbled face.

'Thunder and Jeezus! Nice talking with you but I gotta go. I'm starting a job in the cannery on Monday. If it's still available, that is.'

He hobbles back the way he came. He begins to speed up, and slowly disappears out of sight. I stare after him and I move away from the railing.

Almost regretfully, I begin walking back to the car. It's going to be a long road ahead.

The Change

It is The Change.

When it comes, it comes.
And nothing remains the same.

The Change changes all things
Except The Change.

Mountains melt
And all you felt
withheld
by The Change
Remorseless
Uncaring
Unstoppable.

It is The Change.
When it comes, it comes
And where it goes, nobody knows
Not even The Change will divulge it.

Mosquito Enlightenment

They say that once you transcend a limit, the Universe immediately tests you to determine the depth of your understanding, only to heave you back into the oven if the clay has not been fired sufficiently.

But I digress.

I am on an Enlightenment Intensive — four days of deprivation and inquiry designed to root out the seeds of illusion from the mirror of the unblemished mind.

At the outset, we are told that one of the dozen or so participants has AIDS, we don't know which one. Of course, we all make a show of our magnanimity because we are on the Endless Journey deep into the Selfless One.

After days of examination and insight, I am ready for the test, or so I think. A mosquito alights on my forearm and begins to draw blood. My blood.

Ignoring the impulse to swat it outright, a wave of bliss washes over me. 'Take it! Take it!!!', I say to the little creature. And she isn't asking.

With pomp and smug self-righteousness, I settle back into my contemplation, until the Devil comes a-knocking. 'But can mosquitoes spread AIDS-tainted blood? Have I signed my own death warrant???'

Good questions, but they immediately knock me off the mountain, plummeting into the abyss below.

The rest of the intensive is wasted. And they don't give refunds.

Merrily, Merrily...

My buddy and fellow jamster and I, Richard, were sitting around talking about the nature of reality as usual. His position was that reality is just a projection of the One Consciousness that we all are.

As such, life is a creative act driven by desire, the infinite impulse to evolution and self awareness.

Mine was that it is what it is and no more.

We batted these ideas back and forth for months. Until I had a dream.
Richard and I are walking in a spiritual procession, dressed from head to foot in religious regalia, with heavenly music playing, sacred elephants and tigers and bears alongside us. We are high priests, with adoring crowds and great fanfare all around.

He turned to me and smiled.

'Who are you now, Ross?'

A chill went up my spine and I began to chant.

Epitaph

We spend an inordinate amount of time carving our very small epitaphs, cutting little pieces out of the stone, blemishing the majesty of who we always are.

"Sometimes I go about in pity for myself, and all the while, a great wind carries me across the sky." - Ojibwa

The Sound of Silence

According to Science:
Tinnitus involves the annoying sensation of hearing sound when no external sound is present. Tinnitus symptoms include these types of phantom noises in your ears such as:
Ringing
Buzzing
Roaring
Clicking
Hissing

According to Led Zeppelin:
Your head is humming and it won't go. In case you don't know, the Piper's calling you to join him.

And I lay my body down for a quick nap. In the background were cars and people in the street, music in the distance wafting with the breeze. In the space between waking and dreamland, I became aware of something else.

Absolutely nothing.

It started as a vacuous echo, no-sound piled upon no-sound - so inaudible I scarcely didn't hear it at all, if you catch my meaning.

The fabric, it seemed, upon which all sounds rested, woven throughout perceptible existence. As I focused, the sound became more pronounced, a slight humming at first, then louder and louder, until it consumed every other in a crescendo, a cacophony, a vibration that shook the foundations of Heaven and Earth.

I became afraid; perhaps I would be annihilated. And so it came to pass.

I became aware that a coil of energy was gathering at the base of my spine, and I shivered and shook as it arose at the speed of consciousness and pulverized the Universe until that mask was destroyed and had fallen away, leaving only a few tawdry remnants, and even those were in tatters.

That's when I realized that there are two paths leading to the same place. I'm not certain I ever came back. In this place I received my sacred name; Eagle Two Rivers, I was called.

And the sacrificial waters have been wending their way according to their nature ever since, bearing me home again.

Who We Are Not

What anybody else thinks

The body

The thoughts

The emotions

What we think we own when we own nothing

The reputation

What happens

Looking great publicly

Facebook Likes

Penis/breast implant size

Stories about what an amazing caring person
each of us is

Who we know & who likes us

Anything that changes

The essential issue is whether one thinks one exists as a separate being, which is actually only a small bubble of momentary effervescence, when we are everything and more. We will pummel ourselves incessantly forever until this realization is made manifest.

141

You Will Never Discover the Truth...

...until you tell the truth in your own life. Otherwise, you are living a lie. And the truth has no place in it.

When the Divine Knocks On Your Door

It's far better if you are the one who opens it first.
Before it gets kicked in.

About the Author

Ross Ulysses Munroe is an award-winning creative talent, having served as Executive Editor and writer of a number of periodicals with his wife Virginia, plus a children's book, various screenplays and short stories and more.

He also produces and directs story-driven jazz videos and has received special recognition at the acclaimed NXNE Film Festival. Ross is known for his humor and incisive perspective on the human condition.

Ross' latest work is showcased in his book **First Person Singular**, a collection of short stories, essays and insights certain to provoke and entertain.

From the sordid to the sublime, Ross' writing is drawn from his personal experience, in a delightful and unconventional mix of irony and pathos.

Manor House / 905-648-4797
www.manor-house-publishing.com